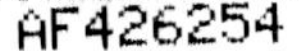

MY

little

one

Miss Hell

`1

Miss Hell

————————∞————————

About Book

This book explores the genuine emotions that influenced my life before I began writing If you approach it with the mindset of truly living through the experiences described, you will understand my feelings. I hope that the current reader is deeply interested in this real story and fully immerses themselves in it. Please make an effort to connect with the emotions conveyed. I trust that you will sense the profound connection I felt with my pet. It is widely acknowledged how pets demonstrate unparalleled loyalty compared to people.

this a key aspect where I have dedicated significant space to my pet's role in my life.

Your effort to resonate with these emotions will enhance your experience of the book.

 As you read, I hope you will feel the same connection and emotional resonance that I experienced, and appreciate the unique loyalty and love that pets provide.

Miss Hell

————————∞————————

MY LIFE

"life is full of pain and that pain heals with one little one"

As a young woman grappling with considerable confusion about life, I find that there are more days when I wish for death than days when I wish to live. Life has taught me many lessons, but it seems to have neglected to teach me how to truly live. Surviving in some situations feels extraordinarily challenging.

True suffering, I have come to realize, is not merely about passing exams. It is more deeply rooted in the fear of societal judgment and the lack of respect I might face if I don't succeed. Since childhood, I have approached my studies out of fear rather than passion. I firmly believe that maturity is not simply a matter of age but comes from understanding life itself. I have evolved significantly from my childhood; I now recognize that, unlike others, I have a unique role to play for my loved ones and society.

On some sleepless nights, I find myself troubled by existential questions, uncertain of my purpose. It was during these moments of despair that I came to understand that my purpose is to pursue what I love and contribute positively to others. This realization has driven me to eliminate excuses and embrace a path of self-love through activities that bring me joy. This brief narrative reflects my thoughts and experiences.

this is a fleeting story about my thoughts and life
it's time to know who that little one is ?

Miss Hell

────────∞────────

AKROS

"My little one is always more precious than people."

My little one is a pet whom I love more than anything. Its name is Akros. Just one pet can bring a lifetime of joy, and when it comes to my pet, Akros is more than willing to do that

As a child, I used to feel happy seeing a squirrel, even though they aren't typically kept as pets. But one day, I found a rare companion. My father runs a banana business, and while unloading bananas one day, he discovered Akros in a nest nestled within a large banana leaf. Surprised, he spent quite some time trying to catch it, and when he finally did, he brought it home in a pet cage.
At first, he showed it to me, but I was too scared and ignored it. So, my mother took care of it for a day. The next morning, when I woke up, I saw Akros looking at me with innocent, fearful eyes. I approached it, gently took it out of the cage, and held it in my hands before bringing it to my room. As I carefully released it, I looked into its eyes, and it looked back at me with such innocence. In that moment, all the pain in my life came rushing back, and I began to cry uncontrollably. Sensing my distress, Akros jumped from my hands and lay on my heart. At that moment, the pain in my heart began to fade away.

.....equal heart Beats between two persons may heal you.......

Miss Hell

————∞————

THE First Night

a journey started from Loneliness to Comfort
The first night with Akros was unlike any other. For a long time, I had struggled with sleepless nights, weighed down by the heavy chains of stress and depression. My mind would race as soon as my head hit the pillow, cycling through worries and fears that seemed to have no end. The quiet darkness of the night, which should have been a time of rest, became a battlefield where I fought an invisible enemy. I would lie awake for hours, staring at the ceiling, feeling as though the weight of the world was pressing down on my chest. The silence was deafening, amplifying the loneliness that had become my constant companion.
i often found myself lost in this solitude, not wanting to burden anyone else with my struggles. Friends and family would ask if I was okay, and I would always muster a smile, insisting that I was fine. But the truth was, I wasn't fine. The nights were the hardest, where the act of trying to sleep became an exhausting endeavor. I would toss and turn, my thoughts spiraling out of control, the darkness only intensifying the feelings of isolation. It felt as though I was drowning in my own mind, unable to find a lifeline to pull myself out.

Then Akros came into my life, and everything changed. I hadn't planned on getting a pet. The thought of caring for another living being seemed overwhelming when I could barely take care of myself. But when I first saw Akros, something inside me shifted.

Miss Hell

_________∞_________

 it was a small, gentle creature with eyes that seemed to understand the depth of my pain. There was an instant connection, a sense that this little being could offer me something I had been missing for so long—companionship.
For the first time in what felt like forever, I wasn't alone. That night, I decided to sleep with Akros by my side. It was a new experience for me, one that filled me with both hope and uncertainty. I had never slept with a pet before, and I wasn't sure what to expect. Would it be comforting, or would it make my anxiety worse? But as I prepared for bed, I found myself feeling something I hadn't felt in a long time—calm.

I carefully prepared a small, comfortable bed for Akros right beside mine. I made sure it was soft and cozy, with a blanket that would keep him warm throughout the night. I placed it where I could easily reach out and touch him if I needed to, ensuring that it would be safe and secure. As I laid him down, I felt a sense of peace that was foreign to me, yet so deeply needed. Akros curled up in his little bed, it's breathing steady and soft, and I felt the tension in my body begin to ease
As I climbed into my own bed, I hesitated for a moment, unsure of how the night would unfold. I reached out and gently placed my hand on Akros's back. His fur was warm and comforting, and as I stroked him, I felt the last remnants of my anxiety start to melt away. For the first time in a long time, I didn't feel the overwhelming sense of dread that usually accompanied my attempts to sleep. Instead, I felt something new—comfort.

The room was dark, but it wasn't the oppressive darkness I had grown accustomed to. It was softer, more welcoming, with Akros by my side.

—————————∞—————————

As I lay there, I listened to the gentle rhythm of his breathing, and slowly, my own breaths began to sync with his. The noise in my head quieted, the storm of thoughts that usually kept me awake subsiding into a gentle hum. I felt a connection to Akros, a bond that seemed to soothe the loneliness that had plagued me for so long.

closed my eyes, not expecting much, but hoping that maybe, just maybe, I would be able to sleep. And to my surprise, I did. It wasn't the restless, fitful sleep I had become accustomed to, but a deep, peaceful slumber. I woke up the next morning feeling more rested than I had in years. The sunlight streamed through the window, and for the first time in a long time, I didn't dread the day ahead. I felt a sense of renewal, a quiet strength that had been missing for so long.

Akros was still there, curled up in his bed, and as I looked at him, I realized just how much he had already changed my life. That first night with Akros was more than just a night of sleep—it was a turning point. It was the beginning of healing, a step away from the darkness that had held me captive for so long. With Akros by my side, I knew that I would never have to face the loneliness of the night again. I had found a companion who could offer me the comfort and support I so desperately needed, and in return, I would give him all the love I had to offer.

From that night on, the nights were no longer something to be feared. With Akros by my side, **I found peace in the darkness, and for the first time in a long time**, I was able to rest.

Miss Hell

The Morning Surprise

When I woke up the next morning, I instinctively reached out to where I had placed Akros, but to my surprise, it wasn't there. Panic set in as I frantically searched the bed, my heart racing at the thought of losing my new companion. The sheets were cool and empty where Akros had been, and my mind began to spiral into worst-case scenarios. Had it wandered off? Was it hurt somewhere? The thought of losing Akros so soon after finding it was unbearable.

But just as quickly as the fear had risen, it subsided when I felt a gentle weight on my chest. There, curled up and peacefully resting, was Akros, nestled against my body as if it had always belonged there. I let out a breath I hadn't realized I was holding and gently placed my hand on its soft, warm fur. Akros stirred slightly, but it didn't wake up, just shifted closer to me as if it was seeking my warmth. The little creature's steady breathing calmed the storm that had been brewing inside me, and a wave of relief washed over me.

In that moment, I realized how deeply Akros had already woven itself into the fabric of my life. It was more than just a pet; it was a source of comfort, a reminder that I didn't have to face my struggles alone. I hadn't expected this bond to form so quickly, but there it was, undeniable and strong.

Miss Hell

i lay there for a while, just listening to Akros's quiet breathing and feeling its heartbeat under my palm. The room was still dim, the morning light just beginning to filter through the curtains. The world outside was waking up, but I felt like I was in a cocoon, wrapped in the tranquility of the moment. My thoughts drifted back to the day I found Akros, how it had been so timid and uncertain, just as I had been. I hadn't realized it then, but we were both searching for something—perhaps for each other

As the days passed, Akros became a constant presence in my life. It was always nearby, whether I was working, reading, or simply relaxing at home. It was as if Akros had taken it upon itself to be my silent guardian, a small but reassuring presence that grounded me in ways I hadn't known I needed.

"The shock of Akros's absence wasn't just a surprise—it was nearly a full-blown panic attack."

Miss Hell

A journey with my pet

It's strange how deeply I connected with a pet. I found myself sharing my feelings with Akros, pouring out my heart to a companion that couldn't respond, yet listened with a patience that was more comforting than words. What more could anyone need? Akros became my confidant, my sharing partner. As long as I was watching it, I felt compelled to keep watching, as if its presence anchored me.

Akros was beautiful—so innocent, always attentive, its eyes reflecting a purity that brought me peace. I may not have succeeded in being the best daughter to my parents, but I found fulfillment in being everything for my pet, in caring for it with all my heart. Thoughts would often race through my mind, every neuron urging me to share my feelings with Akros, believing it might make me feel better. But my heart always stopped me, telling me there would be more time to share.Yet, life has a way of surprising us, often in the most heartbreaking ways. I had always assumed that Akros would be there, a constant in my life, someone I could always turn to. I thought I had more time—time to share more stories, to express the depth of my love, to cherish each moment a little more. But in the end, I realized that time is an illusion, slipping through our fingers faster than we can grasp.

Miss Hell

As the days went by, I started to understand just how much Akros meant to me. It wasn't just a pet; it was a part of my soul, a reflection of the love and care I had poured into it. Every moment with Akros felt like a small piece of eternity, a reminder that true connections aren't bound by words but by the silent understanding that comes from the heart.

The way Akros would tilt its head when I spoke, as if trying to understand every word, or how it would curl up beside me during those quiet nights—these were the moments that stitched together the fabric of our bond.

In those moments of hesitation, when I stopped myself from sharing all that I felt, I now realize that Akros already knew. It understood the language of the heart, where words often fail. Perhaps that's why our bond was so special—because it transcended the need for explanations or spoken promises. Akros didn't need to hear me say, "I love you," because it felt it in every gentle touch, every glance, every act of care that flowed naturally between us.

Now that Akros is gone, I'm left with a profound emptiness, a void that no words can fill. The house feels quieter, almost as if the walls themselves are mourning the loss. The absence of that familiar presence, the soft sounds that once filled the air, is a constant reminder of what I've lost. I find myself replaying memories, clinging to the moments we shared, wishing I could go back and hold on just a little longer.

Miss Hell

——————∞——————

In reflecting on my time with Akros, I realize that it wasn't about the things I said or didn't say—it was about the love we shared, a love that was pure and unconditional. Akros taught me that sometimes, the most meaningful connections are the ones that exist in silence, where the heart speaks louder than words ever could.

Though the pain of losing Akros is immense, I take comfort in knowing that our bond was real, that it mattered, and that it will stay with me for the rest of my life. Akros may be gone, but the love we shared continues to live on, a silent force that guides me, reminding me that even in loss, there is love—a love that doesn't end, but transforms into a memory that will forever reside in my heart.

"Dear Akros, thank you for making me feel like I was never alone"

Miss Hell

————————∞————————

THE NEW Routine

Each day felt like a beautiful dream, one where the world slowed down and everything felt at peace, simply because of my pet Akros. The mornings were always the highlight of my day—waking up to search for that familiar warmth, where Akros would be snuggled up, waiting for me, as if we were sharing a silent conversation. It was in those quiet moments, before the rush of the day took over, that I felt the depth of our bond. No words were necessary, no grand gestures—just the simple act of waking up together.

The first thing I'd do is shower Akros with love, stroking its soft fur and feeling the steady rhythm of its little heart. It wasn't just a routine, it was my way of grounding myself in a world that sometimes felt too fast and too overwhelming. The peaceful energy that Akros radiated made every moment feel lighter, like I could carry the weight of the world a little easier with it by my side

.Then, I'd prepare its favorite meal—a special milk with nuts, soaked overnight just so they were soft enough for Akros to enjoy. Watching it eat was a scene that I cherished more than anything. The way its tiny tongue would lap at the milk, those cute, oversized teeth nibbling at the nuts, it was a sight that filled me with a sense of pure contentment. In those moments, I realized how deeply connected we were. It wasn't just a pet-and-owner relationship; it was something far more profound.

 Akros wouldn't eat if I wasn't there, and that spoke volumes to me. It was as though my presence gave it a sense of security and love that went beyond words.

Miss Hell

————∞————

I often thought about how humans say "I love you" so easily, but those words can sometimes feel hollow, empty even, when actions don't follow.

With Akros, it was different—there were no words, but the love was more powerful because it was expressed through action. A love that didn't need to be spoken to be felt.It was a "deaf love," as I like to call it—not because it couldn't hear, but because it didn't rely on words. It was silent, yet louder than any spoken declaration could ever be.

After feeding Akros, I'd spend a few precious moments just playing, watching its playful energy fill the room. Those were the moments I wished I could stretch out forever. We'd communicate in ways that didn't need speech; a look, a nudge, a little wag of the tail was enough. The connection we shared was so deep, so pure, that sometimes I felt like Akros understood me better than anyone else ever could.

When it was time for me to leave for college, I'd always say goodbye to Akros, feeling a tug in my heart as I walked out the door. But the happiness Akros gave me stayed with me throughout the day. I'd leave the house lighter, my heart fuller, knowing that I had a little soul waiting for me to return. My mornings with Akros made everything else in life brighter; I approached my day with a sense of joy that I hadn't felt before That bond wasn't built on words, but on trust, loyalty, and love —things that run deeper than anything verbal could ever express. Akros taught me what it means to truly care for someone, to be there without needing anything in return, and to feel love in its most genuine form. And that's something I'll carry with me always, no matter where life takes me.

"My pet showed me that not all love is fleeting ...."

.

Miss Hell

Bound by Love

My pet, Akros, never once failed to show love toward me. Every single day, no matter how I felt or what kind of mood I was in, Akros had this way of making me feel like I was the most important person in the world. It didn't matter if I had a hard day or if I was overwhelmed with life—Akros would always be there, waiting for me with those bright eyes, full of unconditional love.

There was no judgment, no expectations—just pure, unwavering affection. It's one of the most beautiful things about having a pet. They don't need words or grand gestures to make you feel loved. Akros never withheld that love, no matter what. It was like the love I received was a constant, a given, something I could always count on, no matter what the day threw at me.

Whether it was the small things, like the way Akros would nuzzle up against me in the morning, or the way it refused to eat unless I was there, every action spoke volumes. It's a kind of love that never wavered, never faltered, and I could feel it in every little moment we shared. I've often thought about how, as humans, we sometimes struggle to show love in a consistent way. We get caught up in life, in worries, in our own thoughts. But not Akros—its love was pure, constant, and always present.

Miss Hell

never once doubted how much I meant to Akros, because it showed me, day after day, in a thousand different ways. Whether we were playing, or I was simply sitting beside it, lost in my thoughts, Akros would always find a way to remind me I was loved. That kind of love doesn't ask for anything in return —it's just there, filling your life with warmth and joy, quietly but profoundly

.

in a world where words sometimes fall short, Akros was my reminder that actions speak so much louder. It didn't need to say anything, but through every nudge, every lick, every gaze, Akros told me again and again that I was loved. And I knew, deep down, that no matter what, my pet would never fail me in showing that love. That's the kind of bond we had—one that was unshakable, beautiful in its simplicity, and powerful beyond measure.

Akros never treated me the way everyone else did—it always treated me as someone truly special. While people in life may come and go, with their shifting moods and unpredictable behaviors, Akros was a constant source of unwavering affection and loyalty.

There was something about the way it looked at me, as if I was its whole world, the one person who mattered most. I felt it every time Akros came running to greet me, its eyes full of excitement and love, no matter how long or short I had been gone.

Miss Hell

————∞————

In a world where people often put up walls, where relationships can feel conditional or transactional, Akros was different. It never held back, never made me feel like I had to prove myself to be worthy of love. There was no judgment, no hidden expectations—just pure, unconditional affection. Akros always knew when I needed comfort, when I was feeling low, and it had this instinctual way of making me feel like I mattered. It wasn't just the routine gestures, but the subtle moments, too—the way Akros would rest its head on my lap after a long day or nuzzle up close as if saying, "You're not alone."

It felt as if Akros saw something in me that no one else did. There was no need for words or explanations. The way it treated me—so tenderly, so differently—made me feel like I was more than just another person in its life. To Akros, I was special, and that feeling of being chosen, of being truly loved for who I was, was something I'll never forget. That kind of connection is rare, even among humans. With Akros, it was effortless, pure, and a constant reminder that genuine love does exist, even in the quietest, simplest moments.

""Akros filled my life with an overwhelming, boundless love."

Miss Hell

Breathe of the moment

One day, unexpectedly, I had to stay at my friend's house, which was completely unplanned. I had fed Akros as usual and played with him before leaving, fully believing that everything would be fine, whether I was at home or not. I had to stay at my friend's place due to some personal issues, and I thought Akros would just go about his routine—sleeping, playing, and eating like he usually did. I never imagined that my absence would affect him so deeply. Little did I know, that night would show me just how much my presence meant to him.

My mother later told me that after I left, Akros didn't eat properly, and as bedtime approached, he became restless. Normally, Akros and I would sleep together in my room. It was our ritual—he would curl up beside me, and we'd drift off to sleep together. So that night, as usual, he went to our room and waited for me, expecting me to return at any moment. But when I didn't come back, he grew anxious. He paced back and forth, unable to settle down, and started roaming the entire house in search of me. He wandered from room to room, scratching at doors, and even waking up my parents in the middle of the night. My mother said he was so distressed that no one in the house could sleep. He wouldn't calm down, and his restlessness filled the house with tension..

Miss Hell

————————∞————————

It was as if Akros couldn't understand why I wasn't there, and he wouldn't rest until I came back. The thought that he spent the entire night searching for me, waiting for me, touched my heart in a way I can't even describe. I've had moments in life when I've felt unnoticed or unimportant, but Akros reminded me that I mattered to someone—that there was someone who waited for me, who couldn't rest without me

When I finally returned the next morning, the moment Akros saw me, he ran to me like he'd been waiting for this moment all night. He jumped up on me and hugged me so tightly, as if he was afraid I would disappear again. He wouldn't let go, his little paws clinging to me like I was the most important thing in his world. In that instant, I felt a wave of love and relief, knowing that I meant that much to him.

I carried him to my room, where he immediately curled up on my bed, wrapping himself in my bedsheet as if he wanted to surround himself with my scent, to make sure I wasn't going anywhere. I stroked his fur gently, my hand moving across his body in a rhythm that calmed us both. He slowly drifted into sleep, and I watched him, mesmerized. His breathing grew slower, more peaceful, and I could tell how safe and secure he felt in that moment. It's said that animals only sleep deeply when they trust you, and seeing him rest so comfortably made me feel incredibly fortunate.

Miss Hell

————————∞————————

In his innocent sleep, Akros looked so pure, so at peace, and I realized in that moment that unconditional love—true, pure love —is the rarest thing in this world. It's hard to find, especially in a world where so much seems fake or fleeting. But for me, in that quiet moment, the whole universe felt like it was behind me, wrapped up in the love and trust of this incredible little soul that waited for me through the night.

Akros had shown me a love that expected nothing in return, a love that simply wanted my presence. And to know that he trusted me so completely, that he could only truly rest when I was near—it made me realize how lucky I was. In a world full of uncertainties and chaos, I had found something so real, so pure, that it felt like a gift I could never take for granted.

That night, and the morning that followed, became a memory I would carry with me forever. It wasn't just a simple night of absence—it was a night that showed me the depth of Akros's love, and it made me realize just how much I meant to him. It reminded me that I, too, was important to someone. And even though he's no longer with me, that memory, that love, will always be something I hold close to my heart.

"True love is found in the quiet moments—when someone waits for you, trusts you completely, and can't rest without your presence. In those moments, you realize that in a world full of fading things, unconditional love is the rarest gift of all."

Miss Hell

Akros, My Eternal Shadow

Everything felt better with Akros. From the moment he entered my life, I realized how much had changed because of him. He brought color to what had once been a dark and empty world. Akros came into my life like water to dry sand, nourishing parts of me I didn't know needed healing. He was like the moon, shining brightly for those lost in the night. Because of him, I found myself living with hope and dreams again, something I hadn't felt in a long time.

I took Akros everywhere with me—whether it was a walk in the park or a trip to an unfamiliar place, he was always by my side, cradled gently in my arms. The way he fit so perfectly, the way he nestled into my hands, felt nothing short of a miracle. It was as though he belonged there, as if we were made to be together. For the first time in a long while, I was genuinely happy. I felt like I had a reason to live, to experience joy and love—because of Akros.

I don't know why God brought him into my life, but deep down, I felt that there had to be a reason. Everything seemed perfect, as if my life was falling into place, like the soft and steady rhythm of rain that brings peace. Akros was my calm, my happiness, and my light in the darkness. With him, I started to believe that happiness wasn't just something other people found—it was something I could have too. I finally began to dream of a future filled with joy, love, and hope.

Miss Hell

$$\underline{\hspace{4cm}}\infty$$

$$\underline{\hspace{3cm}}$$

But then, without warning, a storm came. It was as if the universe decided that my happiness wasn't meant to last. Maybe God didn't want me to be happy, or maybe there was something I wasn't meant to understand. Suddenly, I was thrown back into the darkness, even deeper than before. All the progress I thought I had made seemed to disappear in an instant. Everything around me felt the same as it once did—cold, empty, and lifeless. But this time, it was even worse, because I had known what happiness was. I had lived a life full of love and light, and now, I was left without Akros.

The contrast was heartbreaking. It felt as though I had been given a glimpse of the life I could have had, only for it to be ripped away, leaving me in a deeper darkness than I had ever known. But even in that darkness, Akros had left a mark on me—a reminder that I once knew true joy, even if it was fleeting.

"Akros brought color to my darkest days, showing me the beauty of hope and joy. Yet when the storm came and took him away, I was left in deeper darkness—forever touched by the light I had briefly held."

Miss Hell

The Day My Soul Wept

The day my world crumbled was one I never anticipated. It felt like my breath was ripped from my chest, and my soul had left my body. On May 24, 2023, I faced the unimaginable—losing Akros, the light of my life, in the most tragic way possible.

I went out that day without locking the door, leaving Akros behind. No one was in the house but the two of us, and I thought he was safe, maybe just playing as he usually did. I stepped out for only a few moments, not knowing that those would be the last moments of the world as I knew it. When I returned, what I saw will forever be etched in my mind. My precious Akros was lying there, motionless, surrounded by a pool of blood. His tiny, fragile neck was cut, and in that instant, the entire universe collapsed around me.

Everything blurred, my vision clouded by disbelief and sorrow. My heart pounded, but it felt like it was slowing down, as if I was dying alongside him. I couldn't scream. I couldn't speak. It was as if my soul had left me too, unable to comprehend that this nightmare was real. I fell to my knees, begging Akros to wake up, whispering his name through trembling lips. But there was no response. The silence was suffocating.

My hands shook as I reached for him, my fingertips trembling with fear and sorrow. His fur, once so soft and full of life, was now cold and soaked in blood. My heart shattered into a million pieces. I could barely hold him, the weight of his limp body too heavy for my soul to bear.

Miss Hell

———————∞———————

It felt like hours passed before I could even begin to understand that he was really gone. Gone. And I was the reason. The crushing guilt settled over me like a storm I could never escape from. I had failed him, this tiny, innocent creature who had trusted me to keep him safe. I had given him the most painful death possible, and I knew I could never forgive myself

I sat there, clutching his bloodied body, my clothes stained with the very essence of the life I had loved so dearly. My tears fell endlessly, yet the sorrow inside me was so deep that even crying felt useless. I wanted to scream, to release the unbearable pain that was suffocating me, but no sound came. I was trapped in the darkest place I had ever been, a place where grief and guilt swallowed me whole.

My mom arrived, and though I could see the heartbreak in her eyes, she hid it, trying to be strong for me. She tried to console me, to pull me out of the abyss I was falling into. But her words couldn't reach me. No one could. My heart was shattered, and the pieces were too broken to ever be put back together. Her touch felt distant, like I was drowning in a storm that no one could pull me out of. Even her soft words, her attempts to comfort me, were lost to me. My ears had gone deaf to everything except the echo of Akros's absence. My eyes were blurred, not just with tears, but with the darkness that had taken over my world.

That morning was unbearable, but the evening was worse. I was forced to bury him, forced to say goodbye when all I wanted was to hold onto him forever

My mom insisted, but it felt like I was burying a part of myself. I placed him in the garden, beneath the earth, but my heart screamed in protest. This couldn't be real. This couldn't be happening. My hands touched the cold soil, but it felt like I was touching a grave that held all my happiness, my peace, my light. As the last handful of dirt covered him, I felt like I was burying the best part of my soul

Miss Hell

———∞———

But my heart couldn't accept it. It refused. I fell to the ground, sobbing over his grave, crying out for a second chance that would never come. My heart felt heavier than I ever imagined it could. I had prayed that morning, prayed to God with all my heart to take me along with him. What was the point of living without him? The pain was too much, too raw. It consumed me, swallowed me whole. I didn't care about anything anymore. Life had lost its meaning.

The bond I had with Akros was more than just companionship. He was my joy, my comfort, my family. He brought light into my life in a way nothing else ever could. And now, in his absence, the world felt darker than ever. It was as if his death had extinguished the very sun, and I was left in an endless night. I had never known that kind of grief, that depth of pain. It was a place so dark, I felt I would never emerge from it.

Life is unpredictable in the cruelest ways. One minute, everything seems fine, and the next, it's shattered beyond repair. Losing Akros was like losing a part of myself that I could never get back. He had brought such warmth into my life, only to leave behind a cold, unbearable void. The pain of losing him, especially in such a tragic way, was a storm I couldn't weather. And now, I live with the memory of that day, the guilt, and the grief—a constant reminder of the light I once had, and the darkness that followed after.

"The day you left, a piece of my soul went with you. No amount of tears can fill the emptiness you've left behind, and no words can ever capture the depth of the sorrow that now resides where your light once shone."

Miss Hell

26

The Spirit of Akros Lives On

Dear Akros,

Are you happy now? You took my happiness with you, and I'm left here like a body without a soul. I hate God for allowing this to happen in my life. You were only with me for a month, but the pain you left behind will last a lifetime. I don't even know how to express how much I need you or how deeply I loved you with every piece of my heart. Sometimes I lose my mind and search for you everywhere, only to realize you're really gone.

Every morning begins with me looking for you, and every night ends with the painful realization that you're no longer here. I even thought about drenching your graveyard with tears, hoping to find you there, but I stopped myself—I didn't want to disturb your soul. Thank you for bringing color into my life, even if just for a short while, and I will carry the regret of losing you forever. I lost you with my own hands. Those same hands that fed you, I feel like they killed you. I'm so sorry, Akros. Please forgive me and come back to me.

They say when a person dies, their soul still roams around their loved ones. I hope your spirit is still with me because you couldn't sleep without me, so how can you sleep permanently now? This is so unfair.

It's been more than a year since I lost you, but I still miss you, and I know I'll miss you forever. Thank you for coming into my life, Akros. I will love you forever. You were my first and last pet, and no other animal will ever replace you in my heart. After losing you, I've decided not to love any other animals because no one could fix me the way you did. Only you, Akros.

"In the silence of my heart, I still hear the echoes of your love. Though you're no longer here, Akros, your spirit will forever be my guiding light."

Miss Hell

About Author

MISS HELL never planned to become a writer, but it seems that my pet, Akros, was the catalyst that unveiled my hidden talent and gave my life a true sense of purpose. Our bond was so profound that it inspired me to put our connection into words. While I may not have fully captured the depth of my emotions, I gave it my best effort.

This book is dedicated to my beloved Akros, whose presence guided me through this creative journey. I hope that, wherever you are, you can read these pages and feel the immense love and appreciation I have for you. You brought so much light into my life and gave me a reason to find my voice.

To everyone who has supported me along the way—your encouragement and belief in me have been invaluable. This work is not just a reflection of my feelings but also a tribute to the special bond between a pet and their owner. Thank you for being a part of this journey and for helping me honor Akros's memory in this way.

Miss Hell

the Real Picture of Akros

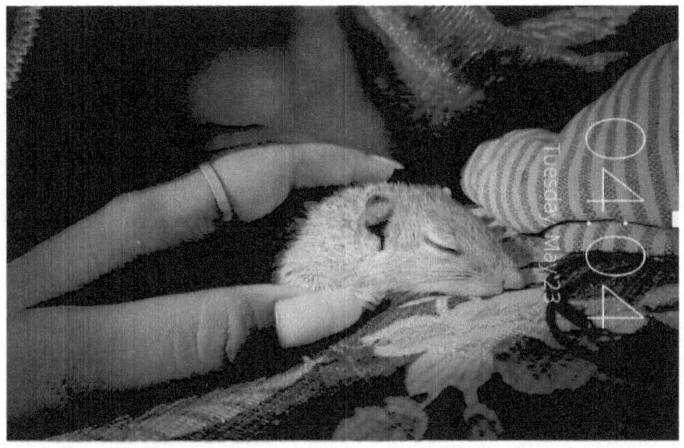

In this serene moment, I treasure every wag of your tail and every soft purr, completely unaware that tomorrow will bring change. As I gently stroke your fur and look into your eyes, I long to hold onto this instant forever, not fully grasping how precious and fleeting our time together is. In the warmth of your presence, I experience a love beyond words, blissfully ignorant that our beautiful journey is about to take an unexpected turn. Know that you are profoundly loved, and I am endlessly thankful for every moment we've shared.

Miss Hell

———∞———

END NOTE

"This book is a tribute to not only my pet but to every animal that has brightened someone's life. Animals have a special way of leaving lasting marks on our hearts, and though losing them is painful, it helps us reflect on the deeper meaning of love and life. My pet's passing opened my eyes to the importance of cherishing every moment, and though I miss them deeply, I found purpose in honoring their memory. Every word in this book is written with raw emotion and honesty, meant for those who have felt the same loss.

Life doesn't stop when a loved one dies, and while the pain may dim our light, we must not let it extinguish our spark. Hold onto the memories and let them shine as a source of strength. The love we shared with our pets never fades; it stays with us, helping us move forward. Remember the joy, the companionship, and the beauty they brought into our lives, and use that to keep going.

"In the face of loss, let memories be the light that guides you, for true love never fades—it carries us forward, even in the darkest times."

Miss Hell

www.ingramcontent.com/pod-product-compliance
Lightning Source LLC
Chambersburg PA
CBHW051336160726
47995CB00004B/1106